Yorkshire Terriers

**Susan H. Gray
and
Warren Rylands**

www.av2books.com

AV² provides enriched content that supplements and complements this book. Weigl's AV² books strive to create inspired learning and engage young minds in a total learning experience.

Your AV² Media Enhanced books come alive with...

Audio
Listen to sections of the book read aloud.

Key Words
Study vocabulary, and complete a matching word activity.

Video
Watch informative video clips.

Quizzes
Test your knowledge.

Embedded Weblinks
Gain additional information for research.

Slide Show
View images and captions, and prepare a presentation.

Try This!
Complete activities and hands-on experiments.

... and much, much more!

Go to **www.av2books.com**, and enter this book's unique code.

BOOK CODE

B475678

AV² by Weigl brings you media enhanced books that support active learning.

Published by AV² by Weigl
350 5th Avenue, 59th Floor
New York, NY 10118
Website: www.av2books.com

Library of Congress Cataloging-in-Publication Data

Names: Gray, Susan Heinrichs, author | and Rylands, Warren, author.
Title: Yorkshire terriers / Susan H. Gray and Warren Rylands.
Description: New York, NY : AV2 by Weigl, [2017] | Series: All about dogs |
  Includes bibliographical references and index.
Identifiers: LCCN 2016004432 (print) | LCCN 2016007006 (ebook) | ISBN
  9781489646019 (hard cover : alk. paper) | ISBN 9781489650238 (soft cover :
  alk. paper) | ISBN 9781489646026 (Multi-user ebk.)
Subjects: LCSH: Yorkshire terrier--Juvenile literature.
Classification: LCC SF429.Y6 G732 2017 (print) | LCC SF429.Y6 (ebook) | DDC
  636.76--dc23
LC record available at http://lccn.loc.gov/2016004432

Printed in the United States of America in Brainerd, Minnesota
1 2 3 4 5 6 7 8 9 0 20 19 18 17 16

072016
071416

Project Coordinator: Warren Rylands   Art Director: Terry Paulhus

Every reasonable effort has been made to trace ownership and to obtain permission to reprint copyright material. The publishers would be pleased to have any errors or omissions brought to their attention so that they may be corrected in subsequent printings.

Weigl acknowledges Getty Images, iStock, Shutterstock, and Alamy as its primary image suppliers for this title.

Contents

Name That Dog

What small dog came from England?

What dog changes color as it gets older?

What dog picks on other dogs ten times its size?

What dog has the nickname "Yorkie?"

There is only one right answer—

the Yorkshire (YORK-shur) terrier !

It All Started in Scotland

Before 1870, no one had heard of Yorkshire terriers. People had other kinds of terriers. Terriers were hunting dogs. Some people in Scotland had "waterside" terriers. These dogs got their name from hunting otters. Otters are animals that live near water. Watersides were small dogs with long, gray coats. People also owned Clydesdale terriers and Old English terriers. These three breeds no longer exist today.

Scotland and England are found on the island of Great Britain. The map on the right shows where Great Britain is on Earth. The map below shows a closer view.

Atlantic Ocean

Scotland

North Sea

Northern Ireland

Ireland

England

Great Britain

Wales

Atlantic Ocean

English Channel

France

Over time, people from Scotland moved to England. Some settled in Yorkshire County. They brought their terriers with them. The different breeds of terriers began to have puppies together. Owners would keep the best-looking babies. When those puppies grew up, they would have babies of their own. In time, these new terriers looked different from the three terrier **breeds**.

In 1870, someone put one of these terriers in a dog show. A news reporter wrote a story about the dog. He said it should be called a "Yorkshire terrier." The name caught on. Yorkshire terriers are still known by that name today.

Soon, people in America heard about these little dogs. They wanted Yorkshire terriers of their own. Today, "Yorkies" are a **popular** pet. They are one of America's ten most popular dog breeds.

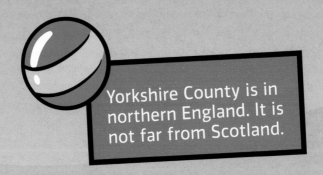

Yorkshire County is in northern England. It is not far from Scotland.

Yorkshire terriers became popular in the 1800s.

Yorkies are so small they can fit inside a purse.

Furry Little Toys

Yorkshire terriers are small dogs. They are about 10 inches (25 centimeters) tall at the shoulder. They weigh about 7 pounds (3 kilograms). That is less than most house cats. Because of their small size, Yorkies are called "toy" dogs.

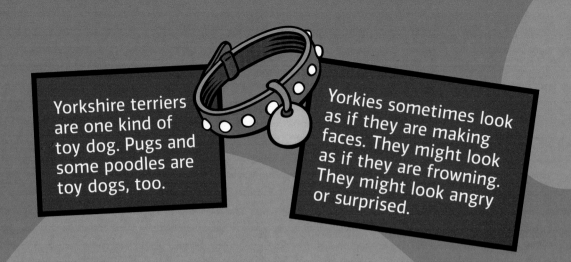

Yorkshire terriers are one kind of toy dog. Pugs and some poodles are toy dogs, too.

Yorkies sometimes look as if they are making faces. They might look as if they are frowning. They might look angry or surprised.

Yorkies are little, but they get lots of attention. People love their long, beautiful coats. Some Yorkies' coats even drag on the floor. They hide the dogs' legs and feet. The hair is long, smooth, and straight. The hair on the head and legs is tan or gold. On the body and tail, it is steely blue. Some Yorkies have darker bodies than others.

The hair on Yorkies' heads is long, too. It sometimes covers the dogs' eyes. Many owners clip the hair around the eyes. Others pull it up into a ponytail. They tie it with a bow.

Yorkies have black noses and dark eyes. Their ears are pointed and stick up. Sometimes, their ears are hidden under all that hair.

Because of their long hair, it is fun to dress Yorkies up. Many owners like decorating their hair with colorful ribbons and clips.

Small, Yet Smart and Brave

Yorkies are friendly, smart, and full of energy. They are sweet and loving to their owners. Sometimes, they try too hard to protect their owners. They might growl and bark at strangers. They might try to keep their owners' friends away. They might try to keep other pets away. Yorkies will snap at dogs much bigger than they are. However, Yorkies can learn, too. They quickly get used to new people and animals.

Yorkies sometimes think they are bigger than they actually are.

Yorkies can play outside, but they get all the exercise they need indoors.

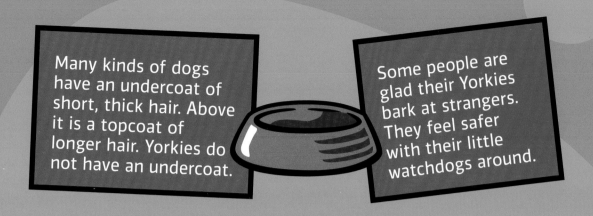

Many kinds of dogs have an undercoat of short, thick hair. Above it is a topcoat of longer hair. Yorkies do not have an undercoat.

Some people are glad their Yorkies bark at strangers. They feel safer with their little watchdogs around.

Yorkies are great pets for people who live alone. They are good for people in small homes. Yorkies like to go outside if they get the chance. They can get plenty of exercise inside.

Some Yorkies can be **stubborn**, but most Yorkie owners say their dogs are great. These little dogs can learn lots of tricks. People teach them to jump through hoops. Others teach them to do "high fives."

Yorkies' size makes them easy to carry around. Some people hold the little dogs in their arms. Others carry their Yorkies around in purses, baskets, or even slings.

Yorkshire Puppies

Yorkie mothers often have two or three puppies in a **litter**. Some litters have only one pup. Others have as many as five. The newborn puppies are black and tan. As they get older, they turn golden tan and steely blue.

Newborn Yorkies are tiny. They can fit in a child's hand. Like all newborn puppies, they are weak and helpless.

Yorkie puppies are so small, they can sometimes fit into a teacup.

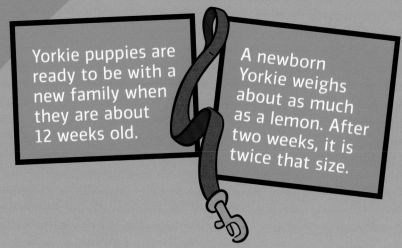

Yorkie puppies are ready to be with a new family when they are about 12 weeks old.

A newborn Yorkie weighs about as much as a lemon. After two weeks, it is twice that size.

Their eyes are closed. Their ears cannot hear yet. However, the puppies can feel things. They can feel their brothers and sisters nearby. They can feel when someone picks them up.

The puppies start growing right away. In about two weeks, they open their eyes. They move around more. By eight weeks, they can see and hear well. They are no longer helpless. They run around, wag their tails, and bark. They are still tiny, though. People need to treat them gently.

These first few weeks are important. The pups learn how to get along with other dogs. They learn how to get along with people. That makes them friendlier when someone takes them home.

Yorkies can go outside once they are six to eight weeks old.

Yorkies at Home and at Work

Many people keep Yorkies as pets. Some people put their Yorkies in dog shows. They groom their dogs so they look their best. They take very good care of them.

Some people teach their Yorkies to be therapy dogs. These dogs visit people who are ill. Being around animals can help sick people feel better. Yorkies are small enough to sit on peoples' laps. They cuddle with people. They do tricks for them. They help people feel better.

The Yorkie's long coats are beautiful when groomed well. These dogs are often entered into beauty contests.

Yorkies are very loyal dogs. Just like Smoky, Yorkies love to take care of their owners.

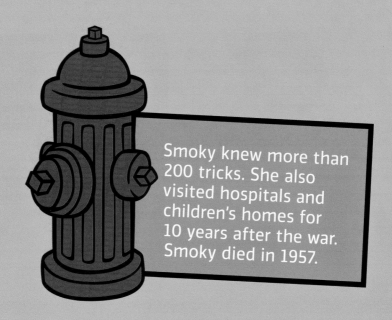

Smoky knew more than 200 tricks. She also visited hospitals and children's homes for 10 years after the war. Smoky died in 1957.

One Yorkie became famous for cheering up soldiers. The dog's name was Smoky. During World War Two, a soldier found her in the **jungle**. The year was 1944. The little dog was hungry and afraid. A soldier named Bill took Smoky in. He fed her and taught her tricks.

Soon, Smoky was showing off for other soldiers. She knew some great tricks. She could even walk a tightrope. Bill trained Smoky to help the soldiers with very important jobs. Smoky learned to do dangerous jobs, too. She became a war hero. The soldiers grew to love the little terrier. Today, people remember her as Smoky the War Dog. In Ohio, there is a monument in her honor.

Due to the Yorkshire terrier's size, owners need to be careful that larger dogs or people do not step on them.

Caring for a Yorkshire Terrier

Two things make Yorkshire terriers stand out. They are tiny, and they have long, beautiful coats. These same two things can cause some problems.

Tiny dogs can get hurt easily. Jumping down from chairs can hurt their legs. Yorkies are hard for people to see. People sometimes trip over them. Children might play roughly with them. Bigger dogs might bite at them. All these things can hurt the dogs.

Some Yorkies can have trouble with their teeth. Regular checkups by a veterinarian can stop problems before they start.

Yorkies need grooming. Their long hair should be brushed every day. The hair also picks up dirt. It needs to be washed often. Some owners cut their Yorkies' hair short. That makes it easier to care for.

Even with their long coats, Yorkies get cold easily. They do not have a thick undercoat like many dogs. The undercoat keeps the other dogs warm. For Yorkies, wearing a coat or sweater can help.

Some Yorkies have knee or back problems. Their kneecaps or backbones can slip out of place. Jumping or playing roughly makes things worse.

Most people take good care of their Yorkshire terriers. They have their dogs for 10 or 15 years. These little dogs live long and happy lives.

Yorkies can be bathed
up to once a week.

Yorkshire Terrier Quiz

Q: Where are Yorkshire terriers originally from?

A: England

Q: What year did the first Yorkshire terrier enter a dog show?

A: 1870

Q: How much do adult Yorkies weigh?

A: About 7 pounds (3 kg)

Q: How often should a Yorkie's hair be brushed?

A: Every day

Q: How long do yorkies live on average?

A: 10 to 15 years

Q: What was the name of the Yorkie who comforted soldiers during World War II?

A: Smoky

Key Words

breeds (BREEDZ): certain types of an animal

groom (GROOM): to clean and brush an animal

jungle (JUHN-gull): a dense forest, often tropical

litter (LIH-tur): a group of babies born to one animal at the same time

popular (PAH-pyuh-lur): when something is liked by lots of people

protect (pruh-TEKT): to keep something safe

soldiers (SOHL-jurz): people who are in the military

stubborn (STUB-born): not wanting to change their opinion

therapy (THER-uh-pee): treatment for an illness or other problem

veterinarian (vet-rih-NAIR-ee-un): a doctor who takes care of animals

Index

Log on to www.av2books.com

AV² by Weigl brings you media enhanced books that support active learning. Go to www.av2books.com, and enter the special code found on page 2 of this book. You will gain access to enriched and enhanced content that supplements and complements this book. Content includes video, audio, weblinks, quizzes, a slide show, and activities.

AV² Online Navigation

Audio
Listen to sections of the book read aloud.

Book Pages
AV² pages directly correspond to pages in the book.

Video
Watch informative video clips.

Key Words
Study vocabulary, and complete a matching word activity.

Embedded Weblinks
Gain additional information for research.

Quizzes
Test your knowledge.

Slide Show
View images and captions, and prepare a presentation.

Try This!
Complete activities and hands-on experiments.

AV² was built to bridge the gap between print and digital. We encourage you to tell us what you like and what you want to see in the future.

Sign up to be an AV² Ambassador at www.av2books.com/ambassador.